The Little Blue Digger

by Harriet Tuppen

illustrated by Branislav Gapic

To get FREE printable coloring pages
of Little Blue and his friends, visit:

www.tuppenbooks.com/freebies/

© 2015 Harriet Tuppen

ISBN-13: 978-1518895869
ISBN-10: 1518895867

For Oliver

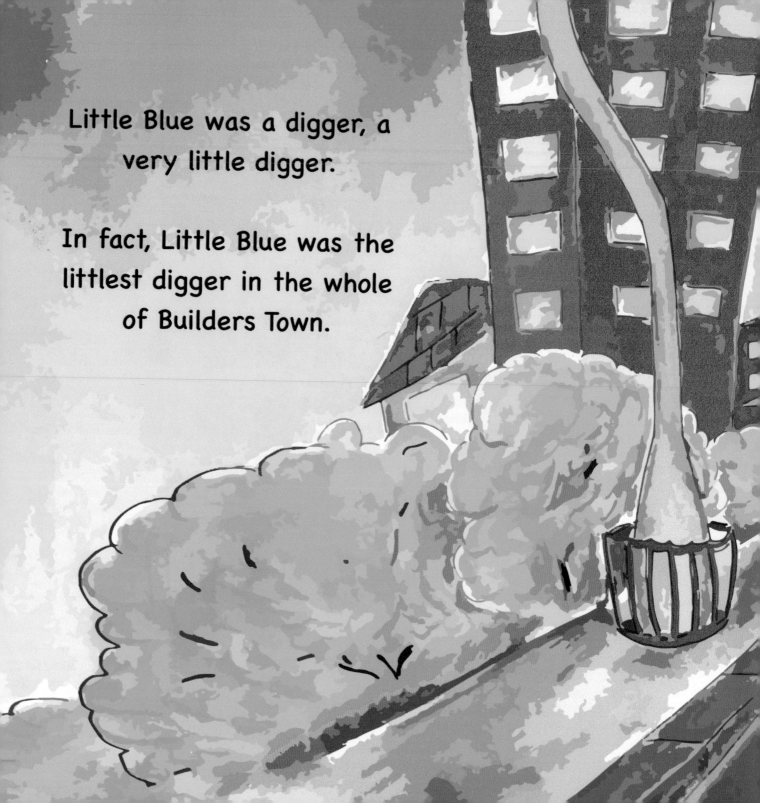

Little Blue was a digger, a very little digger.

In fact, Little Blue was the littlest digger in the whole of Builders Town.

Everyone in Builders Town was very busy building things.

Everyone, that is, except for Little Blue.

"You're too little to help. You'll just get in the way," said Big Yellow.

So every day, Little Blue
watched his friends at their
important work.

Strong Green cleared paths with her sharp blade.

Big Yellow lifted heavy loads with his big front bucket...

...and dug deep, deep holes
with his back bucket.

Tall Orange moved heavy things with her strong, useful hook.

And Wide Red carried
big loads of rocks
and dirt on his
tilting back.

Oh how Little Blue
wished he were bigger
and stronger so that
he could help too!

One day, Little Blue was
watching the work as usual,
when suddenly there was a loud
CRASH!

A pile of blocks had fallen
and trapped Big Yellow!

Little Blue saw that this
was a job for a little digger.
He raced forward to help.

"Stand back, everyone!" he said.

Slowly and carefully, Little Blue started to take the blocks off Big Yellow. His little bucket was perfect for the job.

Then Little Blue's
friends started to help.

Tall Orange gave blocks
to Wide Red to move to
a safer place...

Soon Big Yellow was safe and
Little Blue was a hero!

"Thank you, Little Blue!" said Big
Yellow. "I see now that even very
little diggers can do important
work!"

From that day on, there were always plenty of jobs for the littlest digger in Builders Town!

The End